P9-DCN-412

THE
NEW PUPPY

Story by Laurence Anholt
Pictures by Catherine Anholt

ARTISTS & WRITERS GUILD BOOKS
Golden Books
Western Publishing Company, Inc.

For Claire, who loves dogs

E
ANH

First published in Great Britain in 1994 by Orchard Books

Library of Congress Cataloguing-in-Publication Data

Anholt, Laurence.
The new puppy/story by Laurence Anholt: pictures by Catherine Anholt.
p.   cm.
Summary: A young girl who loves dogs discovers that taking care of a real
puppy involves a great deal of work and love.
[1. Dogs—Fiction. 2. Pets—Fiction.]
I. Anholt, Catherine, ill. II. Title.
PZ7.A58635Ne 1995 [E]—dc20 94-4901 CIP AC

Anna loved dogs.

She had china dogs and windup dogs,

fluffy dogs and bedtime dogs.

She had pictures of dogs on her bedroom wall.

She even had a pair of black and white doggy slippers.

She had every kind you could think of except . . . a real dog!

Sometimes Anna would pretend her little
brother was a dog. She taught him to
bark and crawl around on the ground.
Then she patted him and gave
him a cookie. "Good boy,"
said Anna.

But it wasn't the same. Anna wanted a real dog.

Her dad wasn't so sure.

"A puppy needs to be looked after and trained," he said.

"I could help," said Anna.

"It would eat a lot of food and need exercise."

"I could do that, too," she said.

"It wouldn't stay little
for long," Anna's dad said.

"I like big dogs," said Anna.

"You couldn't just change your
mind and get rid of it."

"I know," said Anna, "it'll
be part of the family!"

Wherever she went, Anna looked at dogs. She tried to decide which kind she'd like. Some were

too long

too tall

too loud

too sleepy

too neat

too hairy

too large

too small

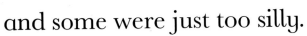

too spotty

and some were just too silly.

One day Anna and her dad and brother went for a walk in the countryside. They saw a field full of sheep and a farmer with a black and white dog.

Suddenly the dog ran across the field and began
chasing the sheep through a gate.
"Look at that dog go!" said Anna.

"That's my sheepdog," said the farmer. "She
helps me on the farm."

"I wouldn't mind a dog like that,"
said Anna's dad.

"Well, come and look in here," said the farmer,
opening the door of a shed.

Inside were six of the sweetest puppies Anna had ever seen.
The farmer told Anna their names:

Teeny

Tiny

Tony

Topsy

Tiger

and Tess.

"They will all need a home," said the farmer.

"Well, I think we could give one of them a good home. Don't
you, Anna?" said her dad.

Anna didn't know which one to choose. They were all so
cute. Then one of the puppies chose her! The roundest,
fattest, happiest of them all waddled across and licked Anna
right on her nose.

"That's Tess," said the farmer, laughing. "I think she likes you."
"Yes," Anna said with a smile, "and I like her. You'll be one
of the family, won't you, Tess?"

But Tess was still too small to leave her mother, so Anna had to wait a few weeks.

It seemed like a long time, but Anna and her brother got everything ready. They found a bowl and made a bed by putting an old blanket into a cardboard box.

WELCOME TESZ

At last the day came. Anna and her dad brought the puppy home.

At first Tess slept most of the time. She ate lots of warm food and made puddles on the kitchen floor, but everybody loved her.

Then she started chewing things . . .

her blanket and her cardboard box,

the rubber gloves and the carpet,

the plants—and even Anna's brother.

"Bad dog!" said Anna, holding her chewed schoolbook.
"You can't eat the whole world!"

Anna and her dad went to the pet shop to buy a proper bed for Tess and something that she *could* chew.

There were all kinds of interesting things for dogs:

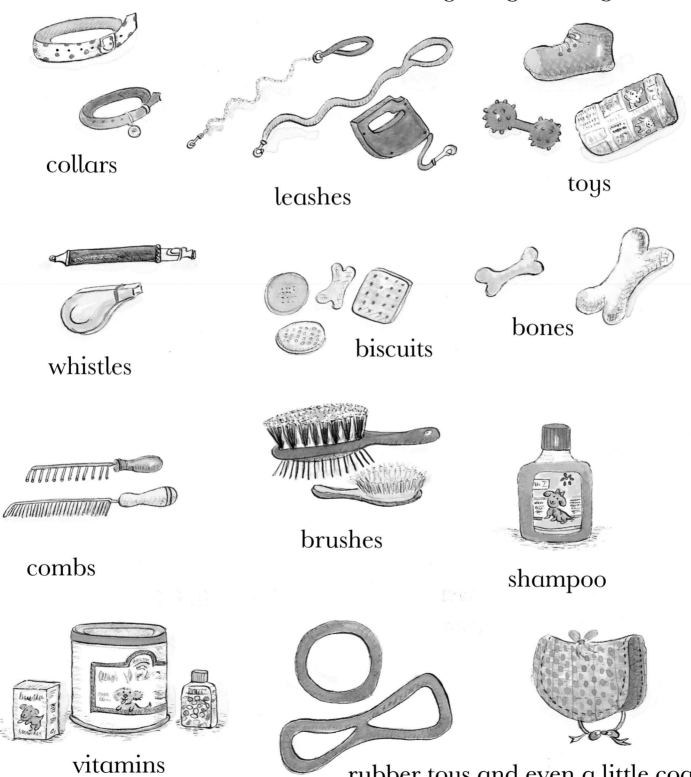

collars

leashes

toys

whistles

biscuits

bones

combs

brushes

shampoo

vitamins

rubber toys and even a little coat.

Finally they chose a big red basket and a squeaky teddy bear,
but when Anna and her dad got home, Tess wasn't there!

They searched everywhere. At last Anna found Tess . . .
in her bedroom. Tess was wagging her tail and looking very
pleased with herself.

Tess had chewed everything!
Anna ran downstairs in tears,
holding the pieces of her
favorite doggy slippers.

"I DON'T WANT THAT DOG!" she shouted.

"She's only a tiny puppy," reminded her dad, "and she's a long way from her mother."

Anna was still very upset at bedtime.

In the middle of the night, Anna woke up. She thought she heard someone crying, but her brother was fast asleep.

She tiptoed downstairs and there was Tess, all sad and shivery.

Anna unwrapped the squeaky teddy bear and gave it to her.

"I'm sorry I shouted at you," she whispered. "I'll be your mother now."

When Anna's dad came down for breakfast, he found Anna and Tess fast asleep in the new red basket.

Tess didn't stay tiny for long.

She grew

and grew

and GREW

and soon she *was* one of the family.

Anna loves dogs.

She has china dogs and windup dogs,
fluffy dogs and bedtime dogs.

She has every kind you can think of. She even has a pair
of chewed-up doggy slippers. But best of all, Anna has . . .

. . . a real dog!

17765

E
ANH   Anholt, Laurence

                The new puppy